A tale for everybody, by Paul Harvey Jr.

E: A Tale for Everybody is a heartwarming story of friendship that teaches children about love and acceptance.

E introduces us to Sara, a precocious and curious cicada faced with the anxious reality of so much to learn and do and so little time. (Cicadas emerge every seventeen years but live only about forty days.) Determined to discover meaning in her brief life and to make the most of the time she has left, Sara becomes enamored of a human boy named Sam whom she has spied passing her ancestral tree and, much to her delight, Sam soon grows fond of her as well.

But the situation complicates as friends and family of both learn of their mutual affection and seem to disapprove. After a while, though, Sara's best cicada-friend, Sasha, puts his own feelings aside and supports her decisions, fearing all along that it can only end in disaster.

But *E: A Tale for Everybody* is more than the wonderful story of a bug and a boy. It is a potential teacher's tool in initiating a discussion about life aspirations and dealing with loss and the responsibilities of friendship. In the tradition of popular children's books such as *It's Okay to be Different* and *Whoever You Are* and *Different Just Like Me*, *E* is something that parents can read to their children, or grandparents to their grandchildren, to help them relate to and respect and even embrace those who are not just like them. Certainly adults without children will enjoy this poignant tale on a different level, although the book should be on every parent's and grade school teacher's "must read" list and is sure to be passed forward for generations.

This is award-winning journalist and Radio Hall of Fame inductee Paul Harvey Jr.'s first children's book.

From the author...

For want of a magical term, we have called them cicada "broods" — uncountable millions of odd looking insects that noisily appear out of nowhere every seventeen years. Their lifecycle is among the strangest anywhere. But they have other secrets...

Almost as inscrutable is this volume, entitled E. For children, it is a story for them. For adults, it is a mystical, metaphorical journey.

Oh, and by the way, look out your window. Open your front door and listen. That distant roar is what this book is all about.

And it's getting closer.

And one thing more: The seventeenth year is here.

~

For additional information, please contact:

Laura Hirschl
PAUL HARVEY NEWS
1035 Park Avenue
River Forest, IL 60305
(708) 366-5371 • (847) 702-9095
laura@paulharveynews.com

E

E

A tale for everybody, by Paul Harvey Jr.

~

Illustrations by Bryan C. Butler

Art Direction by Paul Harvey Jr. and Laura Lulusa

As you read, you may suspect.

And you will be right.

For Dina

*S*ara was born with the knowledge of a thousand generations.

Without being told, she knew to climb, as her ancestors had—and to emerge from her delicate shell, as they from theirs—and to climb higher still, toward the same distant stars, on the same journey that would never quite reach the heavens.

For a *thousand* thousand generations Sara's kind had done it just this way. In fact, for centuries they had climbed *this very oak tree*, even as everything around it continued to change.

But why!

Why climb in the first place!

Yes, to reach the treetop, and to sing, and to attract a mate, and to mate, and to die, but—why!

What was the purpose of all that!

Had Sara's parents known what it was, presumably they would have conveyed that knowledge to her along with the rest. They could not be questioned on the subject, in any case, as they had vanished seventeen years before Sara was born. Along with their entire generation.

So the secret was to remain one, it seemed. Each lonely generation, profoundly isolated from those past and future by gulfs of seventeen years, was simply to act upon the knowledge with which it had been born. And as Sara fretted over that, all freshly undressed and headed for the sky, another question occurred to her:

Why even *make* this journey without knowing why!

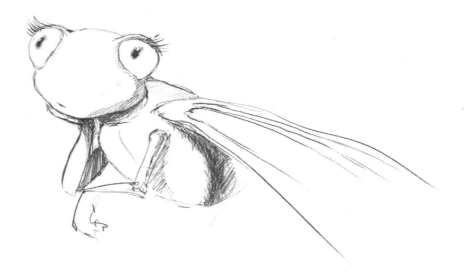

Thus perplexed, Sara stopped. Just stopped right there on the rough oak bark and looked, not upward anymore, but all around her. And it was in those magical, wonder-filled moments that she beheld—him.

Another cicada, like Sara? No, though it would have

made perfect sense. No—he was a boy. A *human boy*, standing below, looking upward into the green labyrinth of the tree to which she clung. Not looking at her, obviously, but appearing to search the leaves and branches for something hiding there.

He was *beautiful*, she thought. Maybe the most beautiful thing she'd ever seen! Not dark and dry-skinned, as she was, but fair. And blue-eyed, as only the rarest cicada. If only Sara had blue eyes, she thought, instead of red, as most of her kind, then maybe the boy would notice her and, better still, would see in her something of himself!

As Sara stared at the boy, it became clear that he was not looking; he was *listening*. But to what! What was *worth* listening to out here in the world of rough bark and credulous climbers! Intrigued, Sara turned to look upward again, but all she heard was the gentle cacophony of nature. The same sounds that had filled the air ever since she had crawled, beshelled, from her womb in the earth. But her curiosity was already beginning to cost her something. Because no sooner did she look back—than the boy was gone.

"Where are you!" she squawked, frowning. To herself, of course. But an answer came nonetheless.

"I'm right here." A cicada voice!

Sara looked up once more to see another pair of red eyes staring straight into hers.

"Sasha!" she exclaimed.

"Your human friend is off down that little path, see?" he advised. Sara squinted past the sunlit grasses waving in the wind to a receding figure. It was the boy, all right. "He lives in that house, I'm quite sure," Sasha offered, "because I've seen him all about the place. It's his 'tree.' Sort of."

"And how do *you* know so much!" said Sara, feeling now as though her destiny, aside from the cryptic cicada ritual, was to miss out on things.

"He has nothing to offer you," said Sasha, trying to smile sympathetically. "He's human, after all. Interested in other humans and human things. 'Curious' is all he could ever be about you."

It was *absolutely humiliating*, the way Sasha did that! From the moment they'd met, rolling forth in that first wave of cicada-kind, he seemed always to be many steps beyond her. Not that Sasha was completely wise. He ought to have known, for instance, that staying quiet is sometimes most helpful of all.

"So what, besides criticism, have *you* to offer me!" Sara blurted out. "A little piece of the pointless lifecycle shared by cicadas everywhere? I mean, we live, and we trowel the foundation for another generation, and we're gone. And *that* you can all do regardless of what or who interests me!"

Sasha was quiet for an uncomfortable minute or so. "Okay, well—maybe you should fly over there and see for yourself. Maybe you *would* be happier there. There are trees around the house. Not your ancestral one, but nice ones. And you're right," he smiled weakly again, "the rest of us can probably spare you."

Gratifying as Sasha's concession was, Sara had heard only parts of it past that business about "…you should fly…" Indeed Sara had never flown! All that consternation about her dull, dull destiny, and she had not even investigated what lay beyond the cicadas' world.

Even as she contemplated the undiscovered discoveries, her translucent, orange-burnished wings stiffened—and fluttered. "See you," said Sasha, turning to climb. Sara answered something, but her thoughts had rushed on ahead to the place where her untried wings were about to carry her.

Hopping off the tree trunk was the easy part. Cicadas are not the strongest fliers, it turns out—a fact for which Sara was fortunately prepared. Still, it was quite a thrill, dropping down a bit into a cushion of air and then rebounding, only to be buffeted by the most innocent breeze. Higher is better, Sara reasoned. Greater margin for error. So up she flew, occasionally letting the playful air currents have their way and slipping past them when they became distracted. Up she flew. And away.

Toward the nearby house.

~

*S*am had just reached the yard fence when he felt something hit him in the head. Like a little stone, maybe. Which it might have been, except where would it have come from?—*and* little stones don't shriek!

But this one did. Or whatever it was did. Just bopped the boy in the head and gave a small, shrill squeal. Sam wheeled around, but saw nothing that would explain the odd occurrence—until he looked on his shoulder.

It was a bug! A charcoal-colored, red-eyed, orange-winged insect apparently stunned and hanging on for dear life. Well, that explained it. Sam had watched the cicadas recent summer days—had observed them struggling from their amber shells and climbing and eventually flying, which for them was more like staggering through the air. It was only a matter of time, he supposed, before one of them accidentally crashed into him.

Aside from what he'd seen, Sam knew only one thing about cicadas: They didn't bite. Or *couldn't* bite, he'd forgotten exactly which it was, but either way, it meant that rescu-

ing this little creature would risk nothing on the boy's part. So he reached over, offering the platform of his hand to step onto. The young maple in the yard should be as safe a place as any for the dizzy bug—even though none of the trees around the house seemed to have cicadas in them. Why was that, Sam wondered. And then he realized: Those trees must have been planted after the last cicada cycle, sometime over the past seventeen years. The cicadas he'd seen were in the old grove. So—was that where this one had come from? And if so—why!

It was not an answer, but it was the closest thing to one Sam could expect—when the cicada on his shoulder bravely—even eagerly?—marched onto his extended fingers, and turned, and—could it be?—looked up at him!

At that moment, for some indefinable reason, Sam began thinking of this awkward, obviously courageous insect as—*she*. What was *she* looking at, he thought. Not at him, surely. But wait!—as he lifted his hand, more precisely to examine this curious phenomenon, Sam noticed—*she*, on the feather-light feet of a tiny ballerina, repositioned herself—as though determined to maintain the most favorable vantage point from which to gaze at him! In fact—were her eyes following him? *Could* they even. In a rush of amusement and warm feelings, the boy took the forefinger of his other hand

and lightly stroked her head and neck. It was like fine, dry leather, he thought. But pleasant, in its way, and not at all bug-like. Meanwhile *she* did not move. As though drinking in his acceptance, his affection, which was a ridiculous impression. Or was it.

Sam lifted her closer to his face, to his lips, saying something like, "Hello, girl!" As his hand turned again, if ever so slightly, so did she—evidently the better to see him—and maybe to hear his voice? And then—she chirped! Sam said something else—and she chirped *again*. She was talking to him! And all the while he kept stroking her, and all the while she sat very still. This was impossible, Sam thought. Bugs don't talk, bugs don't relate, bugs don't "know." He was seeing what maybe he wanted to see, or what he would enjoy telling someone else, but after all—this was nature, not a cartoon.

But even as Sam rationalized, something else was moving in him—something ineffable slowly emerging from a shell of its own—a new potential in his young life—a willingness to believe in the moment, no matter what.

~

*S*asha was singing on a lofty branch of his sturdy old oak tree, in the conscientious fulfillment of his purpose, as he understood it—when he looked up and saw another cicada looping and zooming through the air high above him. "Sasha!" a cicada voice called out. It was Sara. His wayward friend, apparently home from her morning adventure. Moments later she was perched beside him, breathless but, for once in her pensive, over-thought life, she seemed unreservedly happy.

"So?" urged Sasha. But it would not take much urging.

"I met him!" Sara gushed. "It was terribly clumsy at first, but we met and we talked and we spent time together…"

"You *talked*?" interrupted Sasha. "How in the world did you do that!"

"Well, we didn't completely understand each other— but we did, really! At least we understood all the important things. And he held me in his hand, and we strolled around the yard, and he showed me his house—from the outside, anyway."

"And that had better be *all* you see of his house. I'm not sure a cicada could survive in such a thing."

"*Now* who's being negative!" laughed Sara.

The truth of it made Sasha smile. "But now what?" he asked. "I mean, if you're so comfortable over there, why come back here!"

"Well, I had to tell someone, didn't I?"

"Look…" Sasha was serious again, the way he got just before a lecture. "You've got six weeks, give or take. Don't blame me for it, I didn't invent the system. But you've got what amounts to forty-or-so days. So…" Sara could tell he was backing off his point for some reason. Maybe he'd finally got the message: Her life was *her* life. "Just be sure, okay?"

"Okay," she grinned.

And as though celebrating this new peace between them, the cicada chorus rising from the old oak rose higher still—like the memory of an ocean swell Sara had inherited from some distant ancestor.

"Louder every day," Sasha reflected. "More and more of us. The sound is growing denser, almost taking a shape."

"Whether you and I are singing or not," Sara observed.

Sasha caught her meaning. "But I'd like to be missed," he said, as much to himself as to her.

"Well—I *will* be," she answered. The thought itself was irresistible.

~

"*P*ass the peas, please?" Mother's voice was like music and she sometimes even spoke in rhymes without knowing it. This was, in a way, the most wonderful time of day—the family around the dinner table, sitting apart but emotionally huddled together, accompanied by warm voices and the occasional clink of forks and plates.

"Did you hear them today?" Dad often set a question before the table hoping to ignite a lively conversation, and more often than not, he succeeded.

"The cicadas over in the old grove?" said Sam. "Yeah, they were noisy today."

"You think it's the heat, or are there just more of them? asked dad. He knew the answer, naturally, but asking was his way of teaching.

"More of them, I guess," said Sam.

"Did you see your flying dog?" asked older brother, not even bothering to suppress a big grin.

"She's not a dog," murmured Sam, a little self-consciously.

"Well, it acts like one!" older brother exclaimed. "Every day Sam goes outside," he told his parents, "this bug buzz-bombs him. Climbs up the back of his shirt and crawls onto his shoulder and sits there panting for attention…"

"That's *some dog* that could do that!" said Sam, trying to diffuse his brother's ridicule.

"How do you know it's the same bug?" asked mother, logical as always.

"There's a little mark—kind of a star on her head. You have to look for it, but it's there. And besides, how many cicadas like to ride around on your shoulder all day. And like to be petted!"

"Sounds like *you need* a dog!" interjected older brother.

"It's quite a song, isn't it?" said dad, deftly short-circuiting the teasing. "I've never heard anything like the cicada song when they've all come out."

It's E," added mother.

Everyone looked up from his plate. "You mean like, *Eeeee*?" said older brother.

"No, the pitch. The note, E." Mother gracefully slid her chair back and stood and walked into the living room a few steps away. A moment later, a solitary tone burst forth seeking every corner of the house. Mother had struck a single key on the old spinet. "That's E above middle C," she called out,

and she walked back to the dinner table and sat down again. "I hear that every day through the open kitchen window. A deep whirring, almost a *moaning* sound coming from the old grove. Not like insects, really, but more like—one huge, beckoning voice."

"And it's always the same note?" asked Sam.

"It's always the same note," said mother.

"Better enjoy it while you can," advised dad, "they'll all be gone not too long from now."

Sam was stung by the words, but he didn't let on. If the cicadas were gone, then *his* cicada would be gone too, and he wasn't prepared to face that just yet. He'd grown happily accustomed to being sought out every day and being showered with so much attention. For the first time in his dozen years, he felt—important. And he didn't want to lose that. And most of all he didn't want to lose *her*. And warm and safe as he felt in the embrace of the people around this table—there was no one anywhere he could tell.

Almost.

~

waking that morning on a limb of her ancient oak, Sara could hardly believe her little red eyes. It was the boy. *Her* boy! He had come to visit her, certainly. Had come all that way, she thought, forgetting that she had made the effort to visit *him* all those days.

Suddenly excited, she rolled off the limb and into the now familiar air-pillow, fluttering her wings until she could lope her way to his shoulder. Once there, she purred her gratitude. And the boy seemed to understand.

But something was different.

A pall of distress had fallen over him—a palpable feeling which Sara recognized from her own gloominess, before *he* had chased it away. But what was wrong! He couldn't actually tell her. Both of them knew that. Even so—he would try.

He offered his hand and she hurried onto it. Then he lifted her to his lips as so often before and began to speak. His voice was soft. Perhaps too soft for her to comprehend even if she *had* known his language. But something terrible clawed its way through the softness. An awareness. A resolution. That they would never be together like this again.

Sara waited for the crush of devastation. But for some reason it didn't come. Had she been prepared for this all along? Had she quietly accepted the impossibility of which Sasha had seemed so certain from the start? At any rate, Sara—maybe stunned, maybe not—just took it.

But even resigned to whatever had come between them, she refused to belie the significance of what they'd had. It had been monumental, at least to her, so nothing less than a monument would do to commemorate it. Something important for the boy to remember her by. And she knew what that was.

Flying from his hand, she made an ungainly glide around the trunk of the tree, searching among the myriad empty cicada shells—for *hers*. And she found it. Light as dandelion fluff, it was easily plucked from its mooring and carried back to the boy. Hovering above his open palm, Sara dropped her amber treasure and it floated gently down. Incredulously he stared at it, and spoke again—thanking her, she imagined. She was still awkwardly treading air when he turned and walked away, his head lowered.

Their parting had come so swiftly and unexpectedly that Sara was not entirely sure it had happened at all. Could she have dreamed it? No, but she could not figure it out either. She must think. She must find an unoccupied branch and sit there until she had thought this through.

So up she flew.

And there she sat.

Thinking.

But not for long.

"Sara?"

It never failed. In her times of most desperate confusion and discontent she could depend on a Greek chorus comprised of one cicada—named Sasha.

"Not now," Sara muttered grimly.

"All right." Sasha turned to go.

"Wait," said Sara, "there's something on your mind and I'm going to hear it eventually so I might as well get it over with."

Sara was right, there *was* something on Sasha's mind, but he couldn't tell her what it was. Probably not ever. On the other hand, there was something she *wanted* to be told, and that, as a friend, he could manage.

"Follow him," Sasha said.

"You saw everything?"

"Follow him and find out what's the matter if you can, but don't let him stop being your friend if he means that

much to you. Life's too short—for all of us—to stop being friends without a good reason."

As Sasha spoke, Sara reflected in disbelief at how readily she had let the boy slip away. She'd been caught by surprise, that was all. And what if she had misunderstood altogether!

"Thank you, Sasha!" said Sara.

And next moment, she was gone.

She flew so high that other tree clusters and other houses came into view, all of them at once separated and joined by the same intermediate things. It made Sara wonder about all the other lives down there and off in the distance, separated, joined, steeped in joys and sorrows. Could her own joys and sorrows be unique in all this?

And then she spotted the boy. He had almost reached his yard, when…

Someone else—from some other yard or some other place—ran to meet him. Someone about his size…

A young girl.

Sara must stay up here, too high to be noticed. But *she*, even from this distance, must notice everything she could. If she stayed behind the boy, she might draw a bit closer, as no stranger would recognize her. So down she wafted—just a bit—just as the girl took the boy's hand and appeared to squeeze it.

And then she saw the girl's face.

More pertinent still—her eyes.

They were blue.

All of a sudden, uncontrollably, Sara burst out sobbing. Why did they have to be blue!—like his!—like the eyes of the rarest, most envied cicadas! Wasn't it enough to steal him? To tear out her little heart? *Did her eyes have to be blue too?*

Sara careened in midair, scrambling to get away—to get anywhere else. She flew hard against the wind, which ironically seemed to be pushing her back to the yard and the boy and the girl and the disaster that had ruined her life. But she would not succumb to the wind. Nor to her whims. Nor to the whims of nature, in whose domain Sara felt least important of all. She would fly hard, and she would fly away, and she would fly far, until she could fly no more.

~

*S*am had almost reached the gate when he heard running footsteps on the path. It was Susan from three properties over. From his class in school. What was *she* doing here! He couldn't talk to her now. He couldn't let her see him now. She'd see *through* him to the dark, confusing and, all right, *embarrassing* emotions that now practically overwhelmed him.

"Hi!" she called out. But whatever her reason for visiting, if there were a reason at all, she stopped, and took one look, and somehow—she knew. "What's wrong?" she asked in an abruptly quieter tone.

Oh, this was awful. Sam's eyes were welling with tears. *No* one should see him like this! But it was too late. He was too fresh from it all. He *would* have said something terse, off-putting, even cruel, and lurched away. But then Susan extended her hand—and grasped *his* hand—and in her face Sam saw, lying naked and vulnerable there, *his own pain*. A minute ago he could not have imagined the circumstances under which the truth of his feelings could be tormented out of him. But now—Who *knew* why!—he was about to offer it up freely.

"She's just a bug, I know that. Can't think. Just does what bugs *do*, just—crawls and flies and—you know. But she *seems* to like me, *seems* to understand me, and—well?..." The words were sticking in his throat. "Her kind—cicadas—they don't last long. It's like a *million* of them come out and climb up in the trees and—a few weeks later you start seeing them lying still on the ground. More and more of them and—I don't want to see *her* like that. I know what she looks like. I can tell her from the rest, and..." Sam choked on the thought, and Susan saw it. She didn't understand it completely, but she saw it nonetheless. And as her already anxious expression wrenched into utter empathy, Sam saw that too. She reached up, hugged him...

"My grandma told me," Susan almost whispered, "that as long as we live there'll be someone we're afraid to lose. But if that *weren't* true someday, if there were *no* one we cared about—wouldn't it be worse?"

Sam supposed he knew what that meant, although it didn't make life sound any happier. There was something else, however. There was another person sharing his bewilderment and his unjustifiable grief. And in that instant—life actually seemed livable.

~

$\mathcal{S}$ara had flown what must have been a great distance, because it had taken a very long time to get here. In fact she had crossed what had appeared an ocean of grasses, or at least something growing, before arriving at this forlorn oasis: a mostly empty barn of some sort, to whose rafters she now clung.

She was alone. At last. Thoroughly, inescapably alone. So alone that it made no sense whatsoever to have built a barn in this forsaken place. No trees for miles around, so no cicadas. And it was eerily comforting to think that here, eventually, she would die, unnoticed, uncooperative to the end in the oh-so-exalted if unknowable Natural Scheme Of Things.

It could not be as late as it seemed, could it? Aching and exhausted from her journey, she crawled to a small window-like opening in the loft and stared up at the glowering sky. Ill weather was roaming the world, she thought, like a hungry wasp whose jaws even now clamped down on her spirit. And the little gaps in the low-hanging clouds, glowing almost white?—made it all the more menacing somehow.

So.

Here she was. And here she'd stay. And everyone, herself included, would be better off for it.

The intruder on this private desolation presented as a sound at first. A dull buzzing sound. Had Sara invoked the long-dreaded cicada-killer wasp? Had she summoned him from his lair somewhere with a mere dreary simile?

And she squinted into the rancid sky and saw…

Oh no. It couldn't be. How on earth?…

Sasha.

Sasha *again*.

Quite impossibly he had found her out here in the middle of nowhere—to "fix" things. Oh, he was a real genius at that! Like when he said, "Follow him and find out what's the matter," that was *brilliant*. But there was no time to complain, she must hide and wait for him leave!

"Sara?"

He was right outside!

"Sara! Are you in there?"

She scrunched into one of a million dark corners.

"Sara, I've got to talk to you. I've got to talk—*with* you. I know you think I've said more than enough during the time we've known each other, and you're probably right—but there was a lot I *didn't* say. So—this isn't about you or what you should do or shouldn't—it's about me. I want to be your mate."

Cloaked in the darkness and obscurity of her hiding place, Sara gasped, her little red eyes growing redder and wider.

"I want to be there for you," Sasha continued, "I want to make everything that saddens and frustrates and confuses you in life, well—*less* so. You're always railing against whatever it is that compels us to conform, but you know?— the song we sing—that one, loud, cicada song that sounds so very different from our individual voices—that's not an objective, Sara—it's a *coincidence*. It's the sound of two cicadas singing to each other, serenading, nurturing, comforting, adoring—times a million! Nobody knows why we do what we do—why life is how it is. We *can't* know. But we can make it a little easier—together. So—what do you say?"

Running away, Sara had thought she'd never cry again. But she was crying again. "Sasha?" she whimpered, slowly crawling out from the shadows. There was nothing more to say. Sasha had said it all.

~

ndeed he had.

Sasha and Sara returned to their ancestral oak. And whereas none of the matters that had mattered so to Sara had changed, each became less important now—as Sasha had promised—because they faced life as two, times a million, singing, playing, smiling, dreaming.

The day Sam and Susan came to visit the old grove brought a marvelous and happy surprise—a friendship among them that would have seemed impossible such a short time before. Susan could scarcely believe her eyes when *two* cicadas zoomed madly, merrily from the treetop and hovered about, buzzing and chirping, then to alight on her shoulders.

Of course, the cycle of the cicadas rushed onward, as it must, and eventually Sasha—and Sara—dreamed the best dream of all, in which everything sad and frustrating and confusing was gone forever.

And the *human* cycle rushed onward as well, and for Sam and Susan it meant this: That time Susan had taken Sam's hand to comfort him?—in every important way, she never let go.

They *too* remained in their ancestral home amid the houses and grasses and trees. And in their *own* house, one day, the two—became three!

Their little boy was seven when he found the tiny box bound with a rubber band. That's right. Sam had kept Sara's shell all those years! And he told his son how much it had meant, and would continue to mean, never imagining the extent of that meaning.

Because you see?—the cycle of the cicadas had come round again. And sleeping in the earth, about to awake, was the *daughter* of a couple you know. She had *blue eyes*, as you might have guessed, and so fulfilled her mother's fondest wish. Not that blue eyes are all that special. But nothing is special, really, without being so to someone.

And as for all who had come before her, when the little girl cicada was born from the ground, to the tree, to the sky, it would be with the knowledge of a thousand generations. And among those memories was—well, who can say? But someday she would look down from her branch and spy—a boy. A blue-eyed *human boy*.

Who will be the most beautiful thing she'd ever seen.

~

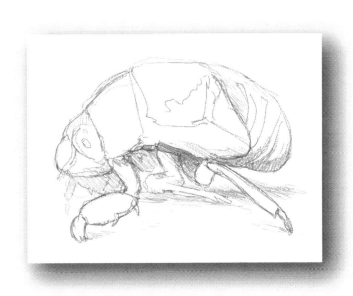